Rob Wilson

For my grandparents

Joseph and Clara Burnham

First published 1984 by Walker Books Ltd
17-19 Hanway House, Hanway Place
London W1P 9DL

©1984 E. J. Taylor

First printed 1984
Printed and bound in Italy by L.E.G.O., Vicenza

British Library Cataloguing in Publication Data
Taylor, E. J.
Ivy Cottage. —(Biscuit, Buttons and Pickles)
I. Title   II. Series
823′.914 [J]   PZ7

ISBN 0-7445-0137-7

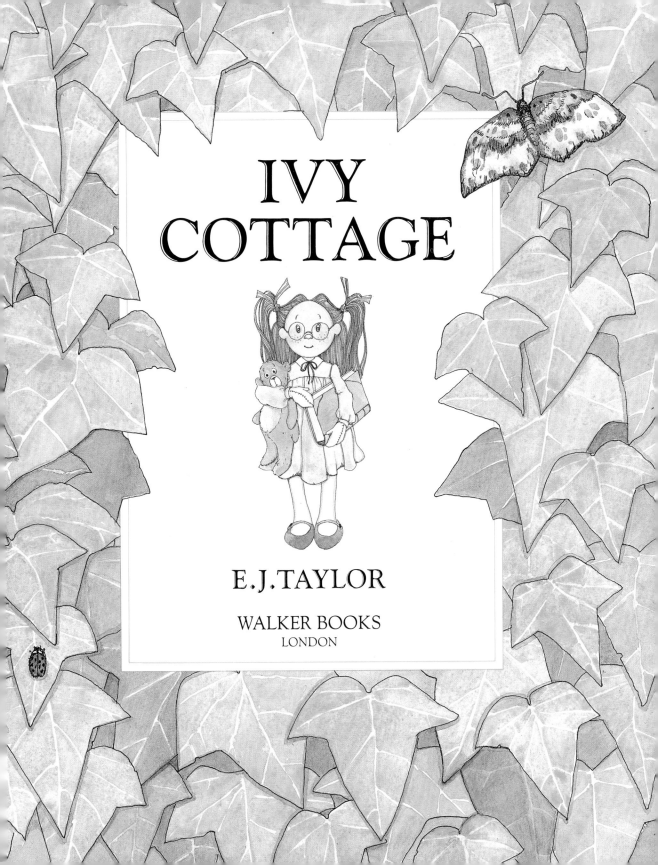

IVY
COTTAGE

E.J.TAYLOR

WALKER BOOKS
LONDON

IVY COTTAGE

For as long as Violet can remember she has lived with Miss Biscuit in the big white house at the top of Primrose Hill. Miss Biscuit is the Nanny there. Violet Pickles is a doll. A rag doll, except she is not an ordinary rag doll. She can write and talk and has very definite ideas about how most things should be done.

Her eyes are blue and she wears glasses. She has long brown hair, which is beautiful, and freckles, which she doesn't like.

Over the years Violet and Miss Biscuit have looked after many children. Miss Biscuit would take them for long walks, prepare their lunch and tuck them into bed at night. Violet would read them stories and give them very good advice.

They were not always happy to hear what she had to suggest, so Violet would say, 'I'm only telling you this for your own good.' And usually, she was right.

It was a way of life that Violet loved and she didn't think it would ever change. But one day, without warning, Miss Biscuit decided to retire.

They were having tea on the porch when Miss Biscuit told Violet that they were moving to the country. Violet nearly fell off her chair.

At first she laughed and said, 'Oh, don't be silly. We have always lived in the city. What on earth would we do in the country?'

Miss Biscuit put down her tea cup and replied, 'I have planned everything. We will live in the cottage that my Uncle Henry left to me. We can buy a goat, and plant a vegetable garden, and a strawberry patch, and some flowers. The country is full of wonderful things.'

Violet couldn't believe her ears. Miss Biscuit got up, cleared the tea cups and took the tray into the kitchen. Violet just sat in her chair for hours and stared at a fern.

Every day while Miss Biscuit packed, Violet tried to persuade her to stay. Every night, failing that, she cried herself to sleep. She soon realised that Miss Biscuit was determined to go and crying only gave her the hiccups.

They left the big white house in a taxi and drove to the train station. Miss Biscuit had two suitcases, a hat box and her bicycle. Violet took a small suitcase, her teddy bear and a picnic hamper, which contained her favourite books, a paint set, a feather pillow, her blue blanket and a silk ribbon.

On the train Miss Biscuit explained their route, adding that she had written to Mr Bickerstaff, an old friend of her Uncle Henry. Mr Bickerstaff owned the general store and would meet them and drive them to the cottage. Violet sat by the window and tried not to cry.

Violet fell asleep. When she woke up the train had arrived at their station. She looked a little puzzled as they stepped on to the platform.

'There's no one here,' she said, and she was right.

They waited patiently for over an hour. Finally, Miss Biscuit stood up. 'I think we had better get to the cottage on our own.'

'But we don't know the way,' said Violet.

Miss Biscuit smiled. 'We'll find it.' And she began stacking their luggage on the back of the bicycle.

Violet looked worried. 'It seems like an awful lot to keep balanced,' she said.

'We'll manage,' Miss Biscuit replied. 'Finding the cottage is our main concern. Let's concentrate on that and let the little things take care of themselves.'

She sat Violet in the basket on the handlebars and off they went.

Miss Biscuit was enjoying the ride. Violet was just beginning to relax when they crossed the bridge and came to a very steep hill.

Down they went, faster and faster. Violet's hair was blowing in the wind and Miss Biscuit nearly lost her hat when, suddenly, there was a loud POP!

'Oh, dear,' said Miss Biscuit. 'I think the tyre's gone flat!'

The bicycle began to swerve and before they knew it, they were across the road and into the ditch and Miss Biscuit and Violet went flying into the air.

'Hold on to my hand!' cried Miss Biscuit.

Fortunately, she had her umbrella, which she opened quickly. She and Violet floated down to a field and landed with a thump.

Miss Biscuit sat up and straightened her hat. 'My goodness,' she chuckled. 'Are you all right, Violet?'

'Yes, I think I am,' was the answer.

'Good, then let's collect our things and be off. We've passed the bridge so the woods can't be far.'

'Oh no!' cried Violet.

'What's the matter?' asked Miss Biscuit.

'Look! The bicycle! The wheel's come off!'

Miss Biscuit turned to look. 'Oh dear. Well, never mind, we'll just have to walk.'

'Walk!' cried Violet in disbelief.

Miss Biscuit stood up.

'Now Violet, try to cheer up and remember, these little trials are sent to test us.'

They reached the woods at sunset and tried to hurry through while they still had some light. The sky grew darker until all they could see were shadows in the trees.

'It's creepy in here,' said Violet and suddenly she screamed. 'What's that over there?'

'It's only an owl,' Miss Biscuit reassured her.

They continued quietly, listening to the sounds in the dark.

Miss Biscuit stopped. 'I can hear the river. See that stone fence: we've reached the other side of the woods. The cottage is up there on that hill.'

They opened the gate and hurried up a narrow path.

'Oh, I can't believe it!' cried Violet. 'We're here at last!' Then she paused. 'Where is the cottage? I can't see anything but trees.'

Miss Biscuit shook her head. 'I don't understand. It's got to be here. It's no use searching in the dark. We'll sleep under my umbrella and have another look in the morning.'

Violet was horrified. 'Sleep on the ground!'

'Yes,' replied Miss Biscuit. 'We brought your blue blanket. It won't be so bad.'

'Won't be so bad!' cried Violet. 'I can't think of anything worse than sleeping on the ground!'

And at that moment, it began to rain.

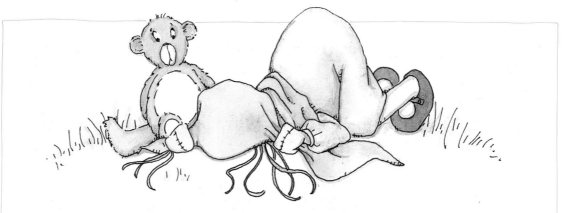

The next morning the sun was shining and birds were singing. However, it was the loud noises in the distance that woke them up. Bang! Bang! Bang!

'We're being attacked!' cried Violet, pulling the blanket over her head.

Miss Biscuit walked to the road to have a look.

Pop! Bang! Hiss! The sounds were getting louder.

Slowly, a rickety old car appeared. There was another loud Bang! and it stopped at the gate.

'Good morning. You must be Miss Biscuit.'

'Yes, I am. You must be Mr Bickerstaff.'

'That's right,' he smiled. 'Sorry I missed your train. This old contraption broke down yesterday on my way to the station. I just got it running again.'

'Oh, don't worry,' replied Miss Biscuit. 'We found the way here, but now we can't find the cottage.'

Mr Bickerstaff laughed. 'I'll show you where it is.'

'Violet, this is Mr Bickerstaff,' said Miss Biscuit. 'He is going to help us find the cottage.'

'Hello,' said Violet. 'It's kind of you to help, but I'm afraid  the cottage has disappeared. Without a home we'll be forced to go back to the city.'

Mr Bickerstaff smiled. 'Look over there,' he said, 'and tell me what you see.'

'I see some trees and a lot of ivy,' replied Violet.

'Walk very close to the ivy and look again.'

'Well, I see more ivy and ICK! three brown ants!' Violet waited for the ants to move and carefully peeked under an ivy leaf. 'Oh dear,' she sighed.

'What is it?' asked Miss Biscuit.

'Bricks,' said Violet, not at all pleased.

'That's it, you've found the cottage, it's under all that ivy!' cried Miss Biscuit, and she began to laugh. 'It was right in front of us all the time!'

'It's going to need a lot of work,' said Violet.

Miss Biscuit stood back to have a better look. 'What do you think, Mr Bickerstaff?'

'Well, first you'll have to cut away all the ivy.'

'Maybe not,' said Miss Biscuit. 'I like the ivy. Why don't we clip it round the doors and windows, and leave the rest as it is.'

'Good idea,' he replied. 'Let's get started.'

In a short time they had pulled away enough of the ivy to open the front door. It was dark inside but Violet found a candle. Miss Biscuit discovered a large pair of scissors in the kitchen.

They opened the windows and snipped away the heavy growth of leaves covering them.

Soon the inside of the cottage was filled with sunlight.

'Oh, it's beautiful,' said Miss Biscuit. 'It's just as I remembered it.'

They explored the cottage from top to bottom. There were dust and cobwebs, but everything seemed to be in working order. Mr Bickerstaff cleaned the chimney and they built a fire. Soon every room was warm and welcoming.

In a few days it began to feel like home, although Violet insisted that her bed was uncomfortable.

They were ready to start the garden when it began to rain. Violet was relieved. She didn't like getting her hands dirty and she could catch up on some reading.

It rained for days and days.

'I'm very bored,' Violet said at last. 'There's nothing for me to do.'

Miss Biscuit picked up her sewing basket, a jar of old buttons, a flour sack and a ball of red yarn. 'Will you excuse me for a while?' she said and walked into the kitchen and closed the door.

Violet was puzzled.

Hours passed. Violet sat by the window watching the rain.

At five o'clock Miss Biscuit came out of the kitchen. 'Close your eyes and count to 10.'

Violet counted and opened her eyes.

Sitting in the chair opposite her was another rag doll.

'She's funny looking,' said Violet. 'What's her name?'

'She doesn't have one yet.'

'I'm very good at names.' Violet thought for a moment. 'She has a button nose and hair the colour of rubies.'

'And rubies are very rare,' added Miss Biscuit. 'How about Ruby Buttons?'

'Well, I guess she is kind of rare,' said Violet. 'All right, we'll call her Ruby Buttons.'

Ruby sat motionless in the chair.

'Do you think she can speak?' asked Violet.

'Why don't you ask her?'

Violet leaned forward. 'Terrible weather we're having.'

There was no reply.

'Cat got your tongue?' said Violet.

Miss Biscuit stood up. 'Don't be rude, Violet. Perhaps she's cold. I'll put some more wood on the fire.'

The log was heavy and it dropped with a thud. Cinders and ashes flew into the air.

Suddenly, there was a loud sneeze.

'Excuse me.' Ruby looked at Violet and Miss Biscuit. 'Hello,' she said, and climbed down from her chair. 'Oh, what a beautiful room!'

'I'm glad you like it. Are you hungry?' said Miss Biscuit.

'Oh, yes, I am!'

'Wonderful. Then follow me.'

The kitchen was warm and full of good smells. There were flowers and candles on the table, with three place settings of Miss Biscuit's best silver and china on a white table cloth.

Miss Biscuit poured some apple cider and raised her glass. 'I'd like to make a toast. Welcome to Ivy Cottage,' she said. 'Here's to Biscuit, Buttons and Pickles.'

And they all sat down to dinner.